GOLDEN FETTERS

AND OTHER POEMS

BY

JOHN LASCELLES

LONDON

KEGAN PAUL, TRENCH & CO., 1, PATERNOSTER SQUARE

1886

CONTENTS.

———◦❖———

GOLDEN FETTERS.

ARGUMENT.

GYNE, having discarded the man of her love, on account of his poverty ; and married a wealthy suitor, for whom she had respect, but no love ; galled by her golden fetters, mourns over the sorrows of her heart.

GOLDEN FETTERS.

PART I.

I.

ONCE again I breathe with freedom,
　　Far from Fortune's false caress ;
Where, it seemed, the hollow-hearted
　　Smiled upon my wretchedness.

Far is now the restless city,
　　With its routs, and with its balls,
Where the stifling robe of fashion
　　Oft o'er hearts in anguish falls—

Hearts in secret ever bleeding,
　　While the stricken strive to smile,
And in mad pursuit of pleasure
　　Seek their sorrows to beguile ;

Where the blooming English maiden
  Oft is sold, like Eastern slave,
Into bondage, dark and dreary,
  Bounded only by the grave ;

Where the sold, and self-abasèd,
  Restless, and with fevered brains,
In the giddy whirl of fashion
  Half forget their heavy chains—

Chains that, to the world around them,
  Seem but ornaments of gold,
But are ever felt in secret,
  Galling, hopeless, painful, cold,

Freezing all life's best emotions,
  Giv'n by God for higher things—
Giv'n that earthly loves might heavenward
  Raise us on seraphic wings.

Oh the crime ! to stifle lovings
  Lent us from the land of bliss,
That its pure and sweet communings
  Sorrowing man might taste in this.

II.

Marriages are made in heaven,
  Doth the ancient saying tell ;
Marriages that are but barters
  Must be made in deepest hell :

Made in regions dark and dreary,
  Where the trembling devils fear ;
Made 'midst demons' mocking laughter,
  Angels raining many a tear ;

Made, with God in spirit grieving
  O'er a soul's relapse from heaven ;
Made, with Satan grimly smiling
  O'er a soul-destroying leaven—

Smiling o'er a kindred serpent
  Coiled around the heart of Truth,
O'er a slow, corroding poison
  'Midst the guilelessness of youth.

III.

Fast the fading leaves are taking
  Changeful Autumn's golden glow,
And a parting gleam of sunshine
  Seems to kiss them ere they go.

Thus the soul of fading beauty,
  Still regretful o'er its clay,
Lingers long, and, in departing,
  Wreathes a radiance round decay.

IV.

Here I sit, 'midst lonely grandeur,
  Looking o'er the wide domain;
And the ghosts of hopes departed
  Crowd around my heart again:

Ghosts of hopes that once were glowing
  For a future, glad and bright ;
Hopes that now have sunk for ever
  Into everlasting night ;

Hopes whose wild tumultuous swelling
  'Tis but left me to forget ;
Hopes whose sad and bitter ending
  Conscience bids me not regret.

Can I say that I am lonely,
  With a husband, good and kind ?
Yes ! that worst of human loneness,
  Loneliness of heart and mind ;

Where the chords of thought and feeling,
  Swept by strange mysterious hands,
Fail to find the sweet responses
  That the yearning heart demands.

V.

Happy were the days of childhood,
    When 'twas joy enough to roam
'Midst the butterflies and flowers,
    In the spangled fields at home:

When I joined the cottage children,
    Wandering o'er the grassy lea,—
Joined them in their childish laughter,
    Sharing all their simple glee;

Till mine ancient nurse would chide me,
    Call me to her side again;
Tell me that "a little lady"
    Should the ragged crew disdain.

Then, I felt, but understood not,
    How convention nature mars;
Felt myself a little captive
    In a cage with golden bars.

VI.

Happier were the days of girlhood,
　　When my heart was fresh and free ;
Dreaming, ever strangely dreaming,
　　What life's casket held for me :

When harmonious thought and feeling
　　Made a music of my life ;
Ere a false world's false ideas
　　Warped them slowly into strife ;

Ere convention's school of folly
　　O'er me cast its fatal spell,
Dragged me from the path to heaven,
　　Drove me down the road to hell ;

When the glowing soul within me
　　Followed nature, true and kind ;
Rose beyond the joys of childhood,
　　To the joys of heart and mind.

Yet, though still my days were peaceful,
  Yearnings of my heart and brain
Made the hidden life within me
  Half a joy and half a pain.

VII.

Happiest days, when first my darling
  Clasped me fondly to his breast,
And I heard, with sweet contentment,
  All his burning love confessed ;

When the chaos of its passions
  Ceased to vex this heart of mine,
Whilst, 'midst music of emotions,
  Came the form of Love divine.

Yes, like music sweetly sounding
  O'er a troubled sea, at rest,
Came a calm, when Love his pinions
  Softly folded in my breast,—

Like the dew of even, falling
　Slowly o'er a thirsty land ;
Or the waves of ocean, breaking
　Gently on a distant strand ;

Like the sound of falling waters,
　On a hot and sultry day ;
Or of Zephyr, in the forest,
　With the rustling leaves at play.

Then life's noblest aspirations
　Rose within my raptured soul,
And there seemed to lie before me
　Something worthy as its goal ;

Climbing, ever upward climbing,
　Towards celestial peaks of light ;
Cheering, counselling each other,
　In a brave and noble fight.

　　*　　　*　　　*　　　*

Ah ! 'twas but a bright ideal,
　Glowing, noble, true, and high ;
But a pure and bright ideal,
　Earth can seldom satisfy ;

But a heavenward aspiration
  Of the godlike soul within ;
But a bright celestial vision,
  Breaking through the clouds of sin.

      *   *   *   *

Yes ! I built my airy castles,
  And, like others, built them high ;
Built them till their highest turrets
  Lost themselves beyond the sky.

And, like builders oft before me,
  On the shifting shores of Time,
Found them based upon destruction,
  Bonded with untempered lime.

For ourselves are but the mortar,
  Bonding blocks that build our lives ;
And the mortar, truly tempered,
  Bonds the castle that survives.

And, I long had lain untempered,
  In a false and foolish school ;
And, in building lofty castles,
  I but laboured as a fool.

So, when storms of fate descended,
   By the blasts of Fortune blown,
Shattered from their false foundations,
   Were my castles overthrown.

     *   *   *   *

Too, too soon, my dream was ended ;
   But, in dreams, it haunts me now ;
And I wake in fevered anguish,
   Sleeping—traitor to my vow.

Yet, 'tis well that once I dreamed it—
   Felt the rapture it could give ;
For my sorrow soon hath taught me,
   Not to love, is not to live.

And, tho' mingled shame and anguish
   Mar that dream I ne'er forget ;
That once I loved, and, loving, lived,
   Still with rapture crowns regret.

VIII.

Often, waking to my sorrow,
  In the morning, damp and chill,
Have I wished the joys of dreamland
  Life's remaining years could fill.

And I trust that Time's impressions,
  In the stainless life above,
Are but blissful dreams eternal :
  Dreams of pureness, truth, and love ;

Dreams, without earth's sins and sorrows,
  Where its tears are wiped away,
And its fondest recollections
  'Midst the chords of memory play ;

Dreams, that for the shrived and pardoned
  Can alone be bright and fair ;
Dreams, that are but pictured memories
  Of this life of sin and care.

IX.

Song.

" Whene'er the carking cares of life
   Around my hearth would stay,
Who soothes my heart with tuneful voice
   And charms its cares away?
           My own true love.

" When darkness, brooding o'er my soul,
   Makes life a troubled dream,
Who best can show me, through the gloom,
   A light celestial gleam?
           My own true love.

" When dark foreboding and distress
   Perplex my doubtful mind,
Who cheers my heart to hope again,
   And is for ever kind?
           My own true love.

"When joys, across my darkened path,
  Like transient sunbeams fall,
Say, who is she with whom my heart
  Most longs to share them all ?
              My own true love.

"When death, at last, mine eyes shall glaze,
  And time its debt shall pay,
Of earthly things, what would I have
  The last to fade away?
              My own true love.

"When sounds the trump that wakes the dead,
  And time shall be no more,
Who would I have to greet me first
  Upon the heavenly shore ?
              My own true love."

'Tis the same—the song he sang me,
  Underneath the starry dome,
Leaning on the ancient dial,
  In the woodland walk at home.

I remember how he kissed me,
  Ere the notes had died away;
All the sweet, tumultuous pleasure,
  As a thing of yesterday.

How our hearts, against each other,
  Beating echoes to the song,
Shared a rapture of contentment,
  As the moments sped along.

Then a thought, too deep to utter,
  Floated dreamlike through my mind,—
But a rapture of emotion;
  Blissful, but to reason blind.

T'was a dream, like voiceless music,
  That our long and lingering kiss
Was a drop within an ocean
  Of eternity of bliss.

But the scythe of Time, above us,
  Hanging o'er the dial plate,
Was the still and stony omen
  Of a swift descending fate.

*　　　*　　　*　　　*

Still we wandered in the woodlands,
  Whilst the deepening shadows fell ;
And we felt a sudden sadness :
  Sadness that was joy as well ;

But a sadness born of shadows
  Closing o'er a happy day ;
But a thought, without expression,
  Joys of earth must pass away.

Then we talked with lowered voices,
  Ling'ring still beneath the stars ;
And we felt the deep emotion
  That the silent night unbars ;

Till the moon arose in brightness
  Slowly o'er the distant hill,
And the dews of night were falling,
  And the wind was damp and chill.

Yet to me 'twas warm and balmy,
  Blowing o'er the moorland wide,
For I had my darling near me,
  And crept closer to his side

Then he wound my shawl around me,
  Pinned it with his jewelled pin,
And, with all his wonted kindness,
  Self-denying, took me in.

X.

I am but a wedded traitor
  When my heart forgets its chain,
And, in fancy, freely wanders,
  Ghost-like, in the past again,—

Round about the ancient mansion
  Of my high and haughty race,
Full of fond associations,
  As my childhood's dwelling-place ;

When my life of self-abasement
  From my mental vision fades,
And again I love and loiter,
  Dreaming, in its woodland glades,—

Haunts that charmed my peaceful girlhood,
  Listening to the cooing dove ;
Haunts that have a dearer dearness,
  Filled with memories of my love ;

Haunts that chainless fancy peoples
  With the lost and with the dead,
Who, in memory's pictured chambers,
  Walk around with noiseless tread.

    *   *   *   *

I am but a wedded wanton,
  When my darling, at my side,
Fondly puts his arm around me,
  Calls me his elected bride ;

Speaking with such sweet distinctness,
  In the echoes of my brain,
That I can but love, and listen,
  And believe him mine again.

XI.

Oh the hopeless, endless anguish,
 Circled by the marriage ring,
When, regretful, fond affections
 Still to stifled memories cling !

Oft I doubt if it be sinful
 To recall a purer life,
Lived before my falseness made me
 A debased and loveless wife ;

But, as oft, a voice within me,
 Like a bell of solemn toll,
Dirging o'er my hopes departed,
 Whispers to my startled soul :

" False, before God's holy altar,
 In thy fatal marriage vow ;
Lingering, longing, looking backward,
 Adds a double falseness now.

" Yet, though lost are earthly pleasures
    By a changeless law Divine,
Strands of gold, to guide thee heavenward,
    Still the kindly Fates may twine.

" But beware, and bury deeply
    Thoughts that warp the moral mind ;
Lest thy soul, though angels twine it,
    Fail the golden chord to find.

" Thou hast sown the seed of sorrow
    In the fatal field of lies ;
And, though but in frolic scattered,
    Seed of sorrow never dies :

" Though awhile it seems to slumber
    In the Lethic dust of years,
Seed of sorrow, sown of sadness,
    Yields a harvest reaped in tears.

" Thou art doomed to endless tossing
    On the troubled sea of life—
On the sea whose waves are passions,
    Raging in an endless strife,

" Till earth's mirages all have vanished,
  And thy vision, clear and far,
With unclouded eyes of spirit,
  Sees its follies as they are ;

" In the day when love no longer
  Shall be false convention's slave,
And the truth shall rule for ever
  In the land beyond the grave ;

" Through the shining pearly portals,
  Shut 'gainst sorrow, sin, and care ;
Where, amongst the changeless angels,
  All is tearless, bright, and fair ;

" In the mystic world immortal ;
  In the world of endless day ;
With a God before whose presence
  Earth's defilements shrink away."

XII.

Happy days ! why were ye fleeting ?
   Days of sorrow, dark and cold,
How I dread ye ! stretched before me,
   With my heart already old,—

Old ! whilst still earth's brightest blossoms
   Should be circled round my head ;
Old, and dead, and burnt to ashes,
   Ere the spring of life has fled.

XIII.

It is well that earthly sorrows
   Cannot penetrate the skies ;
That the peace of heaven is marred not
   By earth's agonizing cries :

For its air is filled with wailing,
   And resounds with shrieks of pain ;
And, it seems, 'midst moral chaos,
   That the Godhead rules in vain

In a world where wrong is rampant,
   And the right, in anguish found,
With the heel of dire oppression,
   Trampled on the bloody ground.

It is well that earthly evils,
   Lost amidst life's closing gloom,
Are, in kindest mercy, hidden
   By the shadows of the tomb.

It is well the blessèd spirits,
   In the land without a tear,
See the good, but not the evil,
   That they did in blindness here ;

And, in peace, can rest for ever,
   Lulled by Lethe's listless wave,
Seeing not their loved ones' sorrows—
   Seeing, when they cannot save.

O my mother! I am thankful
   That you rest in peace on high,
Seeing not the tears you cause me,
   Never hearing when I sigh:

I am thankful that you know not,
   Helpless now, beneath the sod,
That your well-intentioned folly
   Darkens still my path to God.

Mother, you, from childhood, reared me
   In a tinselled world of lies,
Darkly wrapped in clouds of folly,
   Charged with gathering storms of sighs;

And, too late, I see its falseness,
   Lighted by the fires of fate,
In the furnace of affliction,
   When my heart is desolate.

Once, you saw me rise above it—
   Rise to nature, truth, and right;
Saw me make one struggling effort,
   Upward, towards the darkened light;

When, awhile, my heart was lighted
   By the 'nobling lamp of Love,
And I sought, with trembling gladness,
   Mists of earth to rise above;

And, like Psyche in the cavern,
   Went upon my charmèd way;
Felt the Godlike soul within me
   Triumph o'er my baser clay.

Then, O mother, false, and foolish!
   You my treasured secret found;
Ruthless, took the lamp that led me;
   Dashed it heedless to the ground!

I myself was weak and wicked,
   For I took my troth again;
And I see but retribution,
   In a life of ceaseless pain—

Ceaseless pain, and degradation,
   Sharpened, as when angels fell,
And remembered joys of heaven
   Doubled all the pangs of hell.

But I was a simple maiden,
　　Overmatched in worldly art,
Knowing not the subtle falseness
　　Of the marriage-making mart.

XIV.

When the lamp of Love was broken,
　　And my stricken heart was dead;
When Hope lay bleeding in the dust,
　　And the joy of life had fled;

When I cared not what befell me,
　　Since the light of life had gone,
And my path seemed lost in darkness—
　　Darkness darkest where it shone;

Mother! you, with deep designing,
　　Plunged me deeper in despair;
Filled my heart with dark foreboding;
　　Crushed it with a load of care.

Then I took the cup of fashion ;
　Drank it, first, to still my pain ;
But you made me drink it deeply—
　Drink it, till it turned my brain,

Till my stricken heart was maddened,
　And its darkness seemed to blaze
With a host of bright mirages,
　Rising in a golden haze.

Then your fatal work was ended,
　And I did the desperate deed :
Plunged but deeper into anguish,
　Struggling, vainly, to be freed ;

Knowing not the degradation
　Of a loved but loveless wife—
Degradation, dark and damning,
　Ending but with ending life.

XV.

Oh, forgive my lying baseness,
  Husband, ever good and kind !
For the lies of life had made me,
  When I wronged thee, moral blind.

Would to God that I could love thee
  With a love as true as thine !
Would that I could freely give thee
  Half the love that once was mine !

Would to God that I could love thee,
  And could all the past forget !
But my heart is dead for ever,
  And 'tis useless to regret.

Would, then, I could frankly tell thee
  That my life is but a lie ;
Would, that I could frankly tell thee
  And could lay me down and die !

For, in part, I then might free thee
   From the sorrow of my crime ;
And thy life would not be darkened
   By the shadow over mine.

But, though oft the silent reaper
   Finds us 'midst the sunlit flowers,
Oft he lingers, though we seek him,
   When the tempest darkly lours ;

And thy love would then but bind thee,
   Burning like a fiery chain ;
And I long might see thee suffer,
   Ere he made thee free again.

      *   *   *   *

I will keep my guilty secret,
   Since to tell, thy life would mar ;
I will bravely bear my burden,
   Though the goal of life be far ;

Though it steep my life in falseness,
   Though it plunge my soul in hell,
Though my heart be torn with torments,
   I will not my secret tell.

      *   *   *   *

Would to God thou didst not love me,
  Seeking for a sweet return ;
For thy fondness seems to choke me,
  And thy kisses seem to burn.

Oft I feel that I must flee thee,
  Ere the soul of truth expire ;
For I daily plunge but deeper
  In a lake of endless fire.

Willingly, like guilty Judas,
  Would I cast the treasure down ;
All the price for which I sold me,
  Though it were an empire's crown.

I would cast, with gladness, from me
  All the treasures earth could give,
If again, in sweet contentment,
  I could freely love and live.

Nay ! I'd give, and give them freely ;
  Cast them down without a sigh ;
Could I feel that sweet contentment,
  Though I felt it but to die.

*   *   *   *

I could bear, alone, to suffer,
  Drifting on life's restless tide ;
Seeking, 'midst the nameless millions,
  But my broken heart to hide :

But I could not bear to grieve thee,
  And to load thy heart with care,
Making all the life before thee
  But an anguish of despair.

Oh, I could not bear to leave thee
  Tortured with a life-long doubt !
Hopeless ! and yet ever hoping !
  Till the sands of life ran out :

For I know that thou wouldst seek me,
  Anguished with a restless grief,
Till the gloomy lord of shadows
  Gave thy weary heart relief.

Oh I could not, could not leave thee
  To a fearful fate like this !
Yet I dare not linger longer,
  Trembling o'er the dread abyss.

Best, then, I should keep my secret ;
　Bear it to an early grave ;
Best to end a life of falseness
　By a death ignobly brave ;

Best that I should end my sorrow ;
　That my life should reach its goal ;
Best that I should boldly free thee
　At the peril of my soul.

Hark ! I hear a distant footfall !
　It approaches ! It is he !
It is well his sudden coming
　Breaks upon my reverie.

XVI.

It is well that thou hast left me !
　For a fate, beyond control,
Leaves the moments thou art with me
　Traced in stains upon my soul.

Oh this base, ignoble acting
  Of a love I cannot feel !
Oh the anguished, anguished effort
  But my falseness to conceal !

Did I but, like common liars,
  Lie a passing end to gain,
True and sorrowful repentance
  Might efface the guilty stain ;

But this mean debasing acting,
  Silent lying day by day,
With a slow corroding falseness
  Eats the heart of truth away.

Oh, I dread the fearful future,
  With its soul-corroding wrong !
Known, yet daily done, in anguish,
  But my falseness to prolong ;

And in moments, dark with horror
  That my life is but a lie,
I, with such a fate before me,
  Fear to live,—yet dread to die.

For the fate to which I sold me
  Grasps me with an iron hand;
Drags me deeper into falseness,
  Further from the better land.

XVII.

I have seen the wretched outcasts
  In the gay and festive town,
Restless, like afflicted spirits,
  Slowly pacing up and down.

I have heard the hollow laughter
  That is mockery of grief,
When the anguished heart is hopeless,
  And its pain is past relief.

Servants of the mighty dragon,
  They have breathed his poisoned breath,
And, as wages, lie before them
  Hunger, cold, despair, and death.

Who am I that dare despise them,
  Priestly wedded though I be ?
I shall seem but little better
  When men see as God can see ;

When convention's cloak has vanished,
  And the mists of earth have fled,
Frighted from His shining presence
  Who shall judge the wakened dead.

I, the petted child of Fortune,
  Courted, flattered, and obeyed,
Like my fallen outcast sisters,
  Far from righteousness have strayed ;

For, like them, I basely sold me,
  And, more impious far than they,
I, before the sacred altar,
  Dared the bargain words to say.

Oh, I feel the deep debasement
  Of my self-inflicted doom !
And I trust its dark defilement
  Will not reach beyond the tomb ;

But that, in the books of judgment,
  Even sins that most degrade,
When with tears of sorrow blotted,
  From the fateful records fade ;

And that Christ, the Judge of mortals,
  Once a mortal good and kind,
Cleansing my repentant spirit,
  Will but haste my heart to bind ;

Mindful still of human weakness,
  Sympathetic with its pains,
Though above the highest angels
  He in dazzling glory reigns.

Oh, I dare not cease from hoping
  That at last it will be well,
For the torments that I suffer,
  Suffered hopeless, would be hell !

PART II.

I.

Fast the rolling months have vanished
   Since I sat in lonely thought,
Pondering o'er the life behind me,
   And the sorrow it had brought.

Time itself is swiftly sinking,
   In the gulf eternal cast;
Printing man's eternal future
   In the records of the past.

For its moments, as they vanished,
   Graved upon the mind of God
Every thought, of every mortal
   Who this circling planet trod.

And through boundless space around us,
 Vibrate human hopes and fears,
Filled with sympathetic Godhead,
 Far beyond the starry spheres.

Sympathetic! deeply feeling
 Human joys and human pains;
Watching mortals as they struggle,
 Wrestling with their earthly chains.

And, as human wisdom deepens,
 In the glorious time to be,
He shall fill the earth with knowledge
 As the waters fill the sea.

And, though now we see but darkly
 Through the misty glass of Time,
He shall show us in the future,
 Justice, perfect and sublime;

He shall show the why and wherefore
 Of what seems but work of hell;
He shall show, far in the future,
 How He doeth all things well,—

In the bright eternal future,
  When the mists of earth are gone,
And the universe exulting
  Joins the angels in their song,

Heralding a new creation,
  Holier, happier, brighter far
Than when sons of God, rejoicing,
  Sang with every morning star.

I will trust Him ! I will trust Him !
  Though my path be darkened here ;
Though the guiding light before me
  Oft be dimmed with many a tear ;

Looking to the bright example
  On the far Judæan field,
Giv'n when Christ, as God incarnate,
  Brought the balm the nations healed.

II.

Smiling spring, at last, has broken
  All the chains that nature bound
When the dark and dreary winter
  Brooded o'er the iron ground.

Now, the captive earth, rejoicing,
  Crowns itself with festive flow'rs ;
Smiling welcome to the sunshine,
  As it blithely sips the show'rs.

From the upland comes the lowing
  By the distant cattle made ;
And I see the frisking lambkins
  Dotted o'er the sunny glade.

In the trees, the birds are mating ;
  And the flow'rets, as they spring,
With melodious fairy voices
  Seem to ever sweetly sing.

Once again I hear the humming
  Of the lately wakened bees;
Whilst, with soft, seductive whispers,
  Zephyr wakes the slumbering trees;

And a music, soft and soothing,
  Floats upon the dreamy air,
Bringing sounds of glad rejoicing
  Over nature fresh and fair.

Yes! a strain of soothing music,
  Seems to come,—and then depart,—
Soft, and sweet, and sympathetic,
  Waking echoes in my heart.

Well I know, my priceless darling,
  Gently sleeping on my breast,
Why I hear this voiceless music
  Soothing me to peace and rest;

All my inmost soul rejoices
  Over thee, so fresh and fair,
And new life seems now before me,
  And new hope seems everywhere;

And my gladsome heart is singing,
　　Blithely singing over thee ;
And kind Nature, sympathetic,
　　Seems to join me in my glee.

Now, a host of new emotions
　　Pulsate through my wakened soul ;
And, again, life lies before me
　　With a high and noble goal.

I will shield thee from the dangers
　　Darkening still thy mother's way ;
I will point thee ever upward—
　　Upward, towards the perfect day ;

I will point thee ever upward
　　Towards the heavenly peaks of light,
Where the glory of the dawning
　　Breaks the shadows of the night.

I will seek, that I may show thee,
　　Right and truth's eternal laws,
Rising in the throne celestial
　　And the mighty Primal Cause.

Then, perhaps, when life is ended,
  And its sorrows are no more,
I, a shattered wreck, and drifting,
  Still may reach the heavenly shore ;

Finding peace, on earth denied me,
  In the mansions of the blessed,
Where, with the eternal Father,
  All is love and joy and rest.

HELEYNE'S LOVE.

I.

" ERE ten decades have run their chequered course,
So little in thy life's eternity,
Thy love, and all the pangs that anguish now
Thy soul, and lacerate thy bleeding heart,
Will pass for ever into nothingness.
'Twill then be all the same as if thy grief
Had never been ; or thou, with Fortune's smile,
Had clasped thy lost one in a life embrace
Of dearest love and sweetest sympathy."
'Twas thus, with well-intentioned words, they spoke,
Who sought to comfort poor Heleyne, while she,
'Midst all the splendour of her ancient home,
Sat, pale, and listless to the world around,
In silent sorrow o'er her blighted love.

II.

She gave her heart, with all the fondness of
A first, and true, and pure, and holy flame,
To one well worthy of the priceless gift,
To one both good and noble, kind and true.
The fires of genius flashed within his soul ;
And had he found the purest rest of earth,
In heart ennobling and inspiring love,
He might, within the circle of his life,
Have wrought great works of immortality,
And swayed the minds of children yet unborn,
And graved his name indelible
Upon the tablets of a golden age
To be, ere time has run its 'lotted course,
And angel voices usher strangely in
The mystery of eternity.

III.

They walked together 'midst the sweet spring flowers ;
They wandered freely in the woodland glades,
When early leaves were bursting into life,
And mating birds were twittering their loves.

They shared, with simple freedom, all their joys,
And brightened thus each passing cloud of care :
They shared because they could not help but share—
To share had grown so sweetly natural.
With sweetest sympathy they ever joined
In hopes and fears, in pleasures and in pains,
And each gave brightness to the other's life.
From childhood it had ever been the same,
And so, as years rolled on, it came to be,
They knew not, and they scarcely cared to know,
When childhood's friendship blossomed into love.

IV.

A parting first their hidden love betrayed—
Till then a secret unsuspected by
Themselves, that, growing silently with life,
Had been, with youth's unconscious blissfulness,
Locked in the deep recesses of their hearts.
They could not part as friends can part ; they felt
That parting touched them with a hidden pain,
And o'er their lives such deepening shadows cast,
That each seemed walking in an endless gloom,
Of nameless sorrow, brooding o'er the heart.

They knew they loved as man and woman love ;
And when again they met, they told their love,
And felt the rapture of a love confessed.

V.

Alas ! 'twas but of short duration ; for,
Though he was good and noble, kind and true,
He lacked, because his fathers won them not,
The titled trappings of nobility,
That oft are granted by ignoble kings ;
The lands, the castles, and the yellow ore,
That ever, in the estimation of
The baseness of a false and grovelling world,
Are ranked above the gifts of heart and mind
That grant nobility direct from God.
And thus it came to be, for that one lack,
His seeking her was deemed presumptuous crime
By those who thought to lightly barter love,
Like merchants bargaining about their wares,
Or hucksters higgling in a market-place.
And so they drove him from her, and forbade
That he and she should ever meet again.

VI.

And now, poor maiden ! drooping like a flower
That's blasted in the spring-time of its hope,
They think to bind thy breaking heart, and pour
Cold comfort on thy sore and troubled soul
With words like these : "When ten decades have run
Their chequered course, 'twill be the same as if
Thy love had never been ; or thou hadst walked
The bright and sun-illumined path that leads,
'Midst fresh, and sweet, and ever-blooming flowers,
To love's true end of sympathy and bliss,
In marriage, motherhood, and home."
Ah, maiden ! it will not be thus.   They lie,
Or know not all the truth, who tell thee so :
For years of time, that mould for weal or woe
Thy heart and soul, thy mystic inner self,
Like drops within an ocean's mighty brim,
Are but the fractions of eternity ;
And wondrous life to be, when things of time,
And earth, and sense, and earthly joy and pain,
Have sunk into the vast eternal gulf,
Is but continuation of the life

That is, where each undying spirit finds
A passing home in temporary clay.
They lie, who say that *aught* that acts upon
Thy inner self, upon these shores of time,
Can ever be as if it had not been.
Thou art eternal, and thyself must be,
And must remain eternally, thyself,
Scored with the marks of time and circumstance.
It cannot be that things of earth shall cease
To act upon thy soul ; though earth itself,
And all the universe that's seen and known
By those of earth, has passed in flames away.
It cannot be that hopes and fears of earth,
Its loves and hates, its sorrows and its joys,
That once have acted on undying souls,
Can ever cease to act, though angels lose
Their count, and nameless years of time
Are gulfed for ever in eternity.
Thy love, poor maiden, that with torture now
So anguishes thy torn and bleeding heart,
Can *never* be as if it had not been.
A potent cause, it helped to shape and mould
Thy inner self, to make thee what thou art,
And, with effects eternal, still must act

E

For .ever on thy life, for weal or woe.
The loves of earth, that blossom into fruit
Of peace, contentment, and the joys of home,
Give man a foretaste, 'midst the toils of time,
Of bliss awaiting the redeemed in heaven ;
And make him long in that fair land to find
A perfect home, and an eternal rest.
They give nobility to all his thoughts,
And mould a true and perfect character,
Of peace, self-sacrifice, and changeless love,
Unending, in the courts of Paradise,
And that goes with him to the spirit world.
But blighted love debases human hearts,
And turns them ever inward on themselves
In cold, complaining selfishness.
It dwarfs the better instincts of the soul,
And moulds a character at war with self,
With God, with gentleness, and human-kind,
And that goes also to the spirit world.
O maiden, then, cling bravely to thy love !
For it will purify thy heart and soul,
And fit thee for the perfect love of heaven.
Be staunch and true ! for soon, fast fleeting years
Will free thee from the blind and base control

That darkens now the spring-time of thy life.
Take courage, maiden ! thou art not the slave
Of foolish worldlings, or of circumstance ;
Thy life and will are still thine own, to use,
If thou hast courage, as shall seem thee best,
For time and for eternity.
I bid thee, then, in silent patience wait
Until thy years have made thee fully free ;
And then, as thou hast hope of peace on earth
Or happiness in heaven, to leave the wealth,
That might be thine, for other hands to hold,
And yield thy heart, and fervour of thy soul,
To true and free and life-ennobling love.

ANOTHER WORLD; ANOTHER LIFE.

Is there a heaven, a hell, another life,
That must be lived beyond the ghastly tomb,
And that immeasurable ocean, Time,
That surges round, with dark tumultuous waves,
And gulfs for ever from the sight of men,
The hopes and fears, the sorrows and the joys,
The very forms of those they know and love,
And makes them memories of a shadowy past;
Until, at last, it surges o'er themselves,
And all they said, or did, or thought, or felt,
Within the compass of this narrow world,
Has passed away; and fellow-men, for them,
Have drunk the waters of forgetfulness?
Is there a heaven, a hell, another life,
That must be lived, within another world,
When this has passed away, and but its wrecks
Are scattered wide throughout the universe?

Eternal justice, throned within the hearts
Of men, in every age and every clime,
Proclaims there is ; or else there is no God.
It cannot be that God, all powerful,
Looks calmly down, and, all inactive, sees
The righteous weak maltreated by the strong,
Who smile, and revel in their wickedness,
And walk with sunshine on the path of life,
Until they die like other men, and pass
Beyond the reach of retribution here.
It cannot be that God, all powerful,
Looks calmly down from heaven, and sees,
Inactive and unmoved, the countless crimes,
That man commits against his brother man,
That pass unpunished here :
His nameless cruelties against the brutes,
Who, speechless, still are capable of pain,
And which an all-embracing love must bring
Within the universal Fatherhood.
Is there another world, another life,
Where right shall triumph, and triumphant wrong
Shall find a retribution long delayed ;
And all the weak, and suffering, and oppressed,
For faults and follies not their own, shall find

A compensation for their earthly wrongs,
Within a world of universal peace ?
Eternal justice, throned within the hearts
Of men of every age and race and clime,
Proclaims there is ; or else there is no God.
So calm thy soul, perturbèd child of earth,
While gazing heavenward through the mists of time
With eager, anxious, doubtful questionings ;
Another world, another life, is sure—
As sure as that a universal Mind
Created all we see, or know, or can conceive,
Or dream within these finite minds of ours.
For should some vain and blatant fool proclaim
" There is no God ! "
Though revelations of the olden time,
And all that Israelitish prophets wrote,
Or Jesus taught, in the Judean land,
Had never been ; or, in the flight of Time,
The wreck of empires, and the darkness of
The Middle Age, lost to an anxious world,
Had passed again to everlasting night,
And left the sons of earth to seek alone,
Unaided answers to their questionings :
Great Nature, vocal with a myriad tongues,

In earth and in the universe of stars,
Would take again the vanished parable ;
And, waking echoes in the souls of men,
Would answer with an everlasting yea !
And thunder that there is !

THE SIGHTS AND SOUNDS OF
EARTH.

O SIGHTS of earth, that grieve the seeing eye!
And sounds of earth, that shock the listening ear,
Of still and thought-creative solitude!
Men well may feel that wonder, which is doubt,
If it be true that God, all powerful,
Can still be good, and yet, unmoved, can look
In silent calmness down, and see the sights
Of cruelty and woe, and hear the sounds
Of agonized and helpless bitterness,
That shock and horrify the minds of men,
Nor raise the hand of His omnipotence
To right the wrongs, so oft unrighted here :—
The wails of children, tortured for the sins
That others sinned, when they were yet unborn;
The cripples, distanced in the race for bread,
Whose lives are but a long-drawn-out despair;

The maidens, reared without a thought of right,
Or truth, or purity, then harshly doomed,
By cold remorseless cruel circumstance,
To outcast lives of shame and hopelessness,
And outcast deaths, and early nameless graves ;
The righteous poor, oft starving at the gates
Of the unrighteous rich ; the weak, oppressed
And tortured by the strong ; with smiling Heaven,
In silent calmness, looking down the while.
O wrongs ! O sins ! O nameless cruelties !
O sights and sounds and echoes terrible,
That haunt the mind in wakeful solitude,
And fill the night with images of woe !
Faith trembles, and I doubt if it be true
That God is good, and yet all powerful,
Until I go into the still cool night,
And stand alone, and turn from earth and look,
In silent awe, into the dome of heaven,
And see it bright with multitudinous stars,
And know that in that vault are myriads more,
By distance now to me invisible,
And lost in vast immeasurable space,
With all their circles of attendant worlds.
Then doubt is vanquished, and my trembling faith

Is strong ; for then I cannot help but see,
How he is but a blind and crazy fool
Who thinks to judge Eternity by Time,
And God's omnipotence by things of earth.
For standing thus, in awe-struck thought, alone,
The centre of innumerable worlds,
The vast creation starts at once to life,
And night is vocal with a myriad tongues,
And tells how earth is but a speck of dust
Upon the universe of God, and time
A point in His eternity ; and how
In that eternity is time enough,
And in that endless universe is space,
To right the wrongs, and dry the tears, and bind
With loving hands the broken hearts, and heal
The wounds, and ample compensation give
For all the wrongs, of all His children here,
Who suffer woes without their own default.

GRASPING THE INFINITE.

I STOOD and looked into the starry dome
Above me, on a still and frosty night,
And tried, in thought, to soar from earth afar
Until I realized the infinite.
I found the magic of the mind that could,
Within the limits of experience, paint,
One moment, pictures of the distant past,
And, in the next, could compass half the world,
And be with friends at the antipodes ;
Fell dead, when I but sought to rise from earth
And penetrate the mystery of space.
I looked again into the starry deep,
And thought of those I loved, who, dead to earth,
Were living still, and had their dwelling-place
Amidst the wonder of eternal stars ;
And then the magic of the mind returned,

And, in an instant, I could picture them,
Though farther than the smallest star within
The milky way was their celestial home;
And in the infinite I instant found
A resting-place, and lived, in thought, with those,
The loved and lost, wherever they might be.

LOOKING BACK.

I STOOD upon the melancholy ridge
That marks the borderland of youth and age,
And, ere I took a step adown the slope
Of life's decline, that leads to failing powers,
Old age, and that strange evolution of the soul
That men call death, and sadly dwell upon
With childish and unreasonable fears,
I turned, and, looking backward on the road
That lay behind in panoramic view,
And clear in all its winding deviousness,
I saw how often *seeming* trivial things
Had turned my course aside, and made it what it
     was :
The meeting, here, with one who looked a look,
Or spoke a word, that coloured all my life ;
The seeing, there, a scene that struck a chord

Of thought, that in the chambers of the brain
Had wrought, and moulded mind and character.
And marking thus, with vision clear and true,
The turning-points of life and destiny,
I said, "There are no trifles in the lives
Of men! for *seeming* trifles oft are powers
That act, with potent force, for weal or woe;
And what is great or small we know not now,
Or what shall lead to weal or what to woe;
But, in our blindness, this we surely know—
The happiest man is he who, doing right,
With childlike faith goes on, and, well content,
Leaves all the future in the hands of God."

THE BLACK-LETTER BIBLE.

I KNOW a Bible, with its pages worn
　By fingers, that have long returned to dust,
Of men and women with sad hearts forlorn
　But for this book of universal trust
In God, and in an everlasting home
　For men stout-hearted, who still upward climb,
Though oft bewildered, oft they sadly roam
　Amongst the shadows of the " hills of time."
And when I see where men so oft have found
　Sweet solaces to wipe away their tears,
And know them still alive, I with a bound,
　O'erleap the gulf of long dividing years,
And live in loving sympathy with those
Who long have passed away from earthly woes.

THE VOICES OF THE FUTURE.

BROTHERS, do you hear the voices
   That shall rule the time to be,
In the silence of the future,
   Murmuring like a distant sea ?

Onward come the wakening peoples !
   Onward, like a rising tide ;
Onward, with a force resistless,
   Sweeping obstacles aside.

Onward come the wakening peoples !
   Onward, like a mighty flood ;
On to universal conquest,
   Guiltless of their brothers' blood.

Onward come the wakening peoples,
   That shall hold the world in fee,
With the spirit of the ages,
   Leading them to victory !

Will it be for good, or evil,
   That they sweep the barriers down—
Barriers that so long have held them,
   Under prince, and peer, and crown ?

If you want to read the future,
   In the horoscope of Time,
And the destiny of peoples
   As they ever upward climb ;—

If you want to read the future,
   In the horoscope of Fate,
And the destiny of peoples,
   Ere they thunder at the gate ;—

Listen, brothers, to the voices ;
   Listen what the nations say,
As they come from feudal darkness,
   Into democratic day.

Do they say "that self should triumph,
    And that death, the end of life ;
Each should seek his own advantage,
    In a cold and heartless strife ? "

If they do, the devils lead them,
    From the good, and true, and fair,
Onward to a gulf of madness,
    And a shiver of despair.

If they do, the devils lead them,
    Onward to an endless curse ;
And the peoples rule the nations,
    Ruling but to make them worse.

Brothers, listen ! for the voices
    Tell a different tale to me :
I can hear, amidst the chaos,
    "God," "Right," "Truth," "Eternity."

Courage, tremblers ! courage, doubters !
    Jesus leads the coming van,
With a gentle voice, and earnest,
    Preaching brotherhood of man ;

Preaching universal kindness ;
  Preaching universal peace ;
In the wakening of the nations,
  In the fettered world's release.

Courage, tremblers ! courage, doubters !
  More of heaven, and less of hell,
In the wakening of the peoples,
  That is what the voices tell.

THE MONKS' DAFFODILS.

MEN live for earth ; they think for earth ;
   They fret themselves with earthly ills :
And yet they soon are less to earth
   Than trees, and shrubs, and daffodils.

I know a field that, year by year,
   Is brightened by these golden flowers ;
They come with each returning spring,
   And revel in the April showers.

No sign is there that restless man
   A habitation once had found ;
They bloom in lonely loveliness,
   Where nature clothes the verdant ground.

I asked an aged rustic why
   These daffodils were blooming here,
When, searching all the country round,
   No other daffodils were near.

He told me that a priory once
   Stood in that lonely meadow-field,
For friars of the Roman Church
   Their daily orisons to yield.

He said, "In ancient times, the monks
   These beds of Lenten lilies grew,
To deck their church, at Eastertide,
   With symbols, beautiful and new,

"Of that new life and that new hope
   That brightened all our earthly gloom,
When Jesus burst the bonds of death,
   And rose triumphant from the tomb.

"Their church and house, long ground to dust,
   Lie on the neighbouring parish road;
And now these daffodils alone
   Show here was once the monks' abode.

"A living link, they still unite
    The present with the silent past;
They still will live when you and I
    On earthly things have looked our last."

"Then, friend," I said, "why live for earth?
    Why fret ourselves with earthly ills,
When we shall soon be less to earth
    Than trees, and shrubs, and daffodils?"

ELEGY IN AUTUMN.

I WATCHED the setting autumn sun
   Illume with fiery light
The western clouds, to herald in
   The mystery of night ;

I saw the sad and leafless trees
   Stand black against the sky,
Like grim and ghastly skeletons,
   Tossing their arms on high,

As if, in agonies of pain,
   They writhed in troubled sleep,
And wailed their vernal loveliness,
   But could not find to weep.

Then dreamy thoughts passed over me
　　Of mingled joy and pain ;
Like clouds that are touched with sunshine,
　　And colours in the rain.

For I thought of other sleepers
　　Under the graveyard green,
Who had passed, a while before me,
　　Into the great unseen,

No sorrow of regretfulness
　　To break their dreamless sleep ;
For all that earth could keep of them
　　Was wrapt in slumber deep—

So deep, so calm, so beautiful,
　　That like the peace of God
Seemed the sleep that they were sleeping,
　　Under the graveyard sod.

And earth, a mother, lovingly,
　　From dangers and alarms,
But tenderly seemed to take them,
　　And fold them in her arms.

With lingering steps I slowly sought
  The village graveyard near ;
And though the loved were sleeping there,
  I did not shed a tear.

I did not shed a tear for those
  Who, lost a while to view,
Had only journeyed through the mists,
  To scenes of beauty new.

And, as I neared the sacred spot,
  I heard a weird song
Arising from the earth below,
  As if the graves among.

It came, and then it ceased a while,
  'Midst lusty strokes of spade ;
It came again, and then it seemed
  Amongst the graves to fade.

But when, at last, I heard the words
  The agèd sexton sang,
It seemed as if with fellow thoughts
  The very graveyard rang.

For, bending at his lowly task,
    Borne on the sighing breeze,
'Midst strokes of mattock and of spade,
    The words I heard were these :—

" They say that mine's the saddest work
    That ever yet was found ;
To see my friends fall one by one,
    And put them in the ground.

" They wonder that I still can sing,
    A sexton forty years,
When I have dug so many graves,
    And seen so many tears.

" But mine is not the mournful task
    The village maidens say ;
The house is all they bring to me,
    The man has gone away ;

" A crazy cottage, at the best,
    When he was tenant here,
It gave him shelter ; but its walls
    Were stained with many a tear.

" He lived; and here he had his share
   Of pleasure and of pain,
So mingled, and so sorrowful,
   He would not live again.

" They said he died; and yet, to me,
   He only went away,
And still, beyond the shadows, lived
   In never-ending day.

"To me, he only went away,
   And sought another land,
Where friends and neighbours welcomed him,
   A bright and smiling band;

" Where those he best had known and loved,
   Who journeyed there before,
With radiant faces welcomed him,
   To part for nevermore.

" So, thus I sing, and dig my graves,
   Till I shall journey too,
And all the misty shadows hide
   Shall burst upon my view:

" So, thus I sing, and dig my graves,
   Till men shall say, ' He dies,'
And I, no longer lost in mists,
   Shall see realities."

THE VEILED MESSENGER.

I saw a ghostly figure walk
    Amidst the ranks of life ;
At his approach, a stillness hushed
    Its tumult and its strife.

With noiseless steps, and echoless,
    The figure seemed to glide,
As I have seen a shadowed cloud
    Upon a mountain side.

The figure walked so silently,
    His footsteps left no sound,
To tell when he was close to you,
    Upon the awe-struck ground.

But prince and peer, when he drew near,
　　Who never bowed before,
Fell down and kissed their kindred dust,
　　And fell, to rise no more.

A mystic robe enveloped him
　　From head to silent feet;
The figure only lifted it
　　To those he came to greet.

And those he greeted followed him
　　Into the world unseen;
They looked at him and followed him
　　With strangely varied mien.

I saw him raise his robe to those
　　Whose lives were not of God;
They looked at him, and started back,
　　But went the way he trod;

They shrank with trembling horror back;
　　His visage seemed to be,
To them, a grim and ghastly thing,
　　Too terrible to see.

But when he came and greeted those
 Whose lives were good and true,
They smiled, as if an angel face
 Had floated into view ;

Such smiles of radiant loveliness
 As I have never seen
But on the faces of the good,
 When life and death between.

O strange mysterious messenger !
 Who calls to heaven or hell,
With demon face, or angel face,
 As men live ill or well,

May I so live that, when my soul
 Shall greeted be by thee,
Thy lifted robe may then disclose
 Thy angel face to me.

ODE IN AUTUMN.

I STOOD upon a grassy knoll
   Upon an autumn day,
And saw the many coloured woods
   Stretched out in bright array :

The woods in autumn !—beautiful,
   Beyond their vernal green !
With tints of red, and brown, and gold,
   And many shades between.

And yet the woods were dead and cold
   Upon that autumn day ;
The beauty that enchanted me,
   The beauty of decay :

Until a gleam of sunshine shot
　　Along the heavenly height,
And touched the dying woodlands with
　　The alchemy of light.

At once the brown and withered leaves
　　Were bright and glowing gold,
So gorgeous and so beautiful,
　　I could not think them old—

I could not think them old,
　　And falling fast to die,
So gorgeous and so beautiful,
　　Beneath the autumn sky.

And then I said, " O withered leaves !
　　Whose day of life is done,
And yet, who look so beautiful
　　Beneath the Autumn sun,

" My day of life, though more prolonged,
　　Is hastening to its close,
And I, like you, in mother earth
　　Must find a long repose.

" My day of life, though more prolonged,
　　Like yours, is over soon ;
So let me seize the passing hour,
　　When life is at the noon ;

" And when my work of life is done,
　　And I must fall to die,
May kisses of celestial light
　　My dying glorify."

SNOW-FLAKES.

Snow-flakes softly, slowly falling,
   Floating, frisking in the wind,
Leaving, with a half-reluctance,
   Your aërial home behind.

Speak to me in language gentle ;
   Tell me, snow-flakes, what you are,
Falling from the dreamy cloudland,
   From the mystery afar.

" Like the things of life and nature,
   Seen with eyesight clear or dim,
What we *seem* to every gazer,
   That we are in *truth* to him.

"We are but a means of frolic
    To the schoolboy at his play ;
We are curses to the workman
    Doomed to spend an idle day ;

"And to him who skims the surface
    Of the things he sees around,
We are but a general whiteness,
    Covering the naked ground.

"But to him who, looking deeper,
    Sees us truly, as we are,
We are things of form and beauty,
    Each a wondrous little star ;

"We are showers of heavenly flowers,
    Falling from the fields of air ;
Evanescent indications
    Of the perfect beauty there :

"And the lesson we are teaching,
    Ere we vanish out of view,
Is to see in men and nature,
    Not the *seeming*, but the *true ;*

" Looking deep below the surface
   For the beautiful and fair,
With a steadfast faith, and earnest,
   That the beautiful is there ;

" Looking for a soul of beauty,
   Dimly, dimly understood ;
Listening to celestial whisperings
   Of a universal good—

" Good in men, and good in nature,
   Good in life, and everything,
In a universe of beauty,
   And a never-ending Spring."

THE WINTER STORM.

O SNOW, so bright, so beautiful !
  O wondrously woven dress !
Descending from the loom of heaven
  To cover Nature's nakedness.

O forms fantastic ! strangely traced
  By frost upon the window-pane,
And wrought to scenes of fairyland,
  Within the workshop of the brain.

I love you, as I ever love
  The beautiful in land and sea,
And in the cloudy forms that float
  In shapes majestic over me.

Dare I rejoice that you are here,
  Or wish a beauty to remain,
That saddens creatures bound to me
  By brotherhood of life and pain ?

Dare I rejoice? No, no! not so!
For many a bird, with drooping wing,
    And famine in its sunken eye,
Sits sadly near a leafless hedge,
    In silent misery to die.

Dare I rejoice? No, no! not so!
For many a hungry brother man,
    With hungry children weeping round,
Sits listless by a dying fire;
    Starvation in the frozen ground.

Dare I rejoice? No, no! not so!
For, on the crowded road of life,
    Full many a traveller, bowed with age,
Will fall and die, who might have gone
    In peace another easy stage.

Dare I rejoice? No, no! not so!
I dare not sin so great a sin,
    And, bannered selfishness unfurled,
In cruel isolation live,
    A monster in an empty world.

THE DEATH OF LOVE.

O DEATH, supremely terrible
  In any shape or form—
In peace, or in the agony
  Of battle-field or storm !

O Death ! O birth to higher life !
  O gate of the unknown,
That every child of man must pass,
  Mysteriously alone !

We dread thee not for parting pains,
  Or horrors of the tomb,
Thou undiscovered mystery,
  Thou universal doom !

We dread thee not for shutting up
  The fateful book of life ;
For oft it tells a chequered tale
  Of weariness and strife.

We dread thee for the cruelty
  Of life-enduring pains,
Of sundered souls, that Love would bind
  With adamantine chains.

But Love can leap the shadowy gulf,
  If it be strong and true ;
And bind together faithful hearts,
  Though one is lost to view.

Yes ! Love can leap the gulf between
  Eternity and Time,
And bind together faithful hearts
  In sympathy sublime.

    *   *   *   *

There is a death more terrible
  Than death of wife or child—
A death to which the aching heart
  Is never reconciled ;

A death that knows no charnel-house,
  No horrors of the tomb ;
A death in life ; a living death ;
  A dark and hopeless doom ;

A death that sunders human souls,
  And sunders them for ever ;
A death whose ashes of regret
  Can be rekindled never ;

A death whose withered hopelessness,
  Like leaves upon the ground,
The winds of life but sigh upon,
  With sad and sorrowing sound ;

A death that has no recompense,
  In earth, or heaven above :
The death that kills the balm of death—
  The death, the death, of Love.

STRICKEN FACES.

As travellers through a land unknown
    Take note of things they chance to find
That, strange or beautiful, are fit
    To be possessions of the mind,

And stores of thoughts and memories,
    Within the chambers of the brain,
For bankrupt life to draw upon
    And bring its pleasures back again,

So I, a traveller through a world
    Of many-sided life and thought,
Watch faces on whose painfulness
    The agonies of earth have wrought

Sad mirrored pictures of the storms,
  And living records of the strife
Of passions, that have swept the strings,
  Half broken, of the harp of life,

And when I see a face that looks
  On scenes of festival and mirth
With listless eyes, as one who has
  No part in revelries of earth,—

Like some sad soul that gazes from
  The land of hopelessness and tears,
Across the gulf impassable,
  On joys it knew in happier years,—

My deepest tenderness is touched,
  And pity, that is love Divine,
Fans high the purifying fires
  That cleanse the soul, and shine

Upon our poor mortality,
  And make it like to God, and purge
Its dross of selfishness away,
  And with a mighty impulse urge

It forward on the road to heaven,
　　To find, in hope's fruition there,
Where perfect beauty reigns supreme
　　And perfect love is everywhere,

The richest treasures of the soul
　　That live through its eternal years,
Are memories of pity's deeds
　　Done in its pilgrimage of tears.

THE POWER OF LOVE.

I saw a lyre in a neglected room,
Its music mute, and dust upon its strings ;
And all around it were insensate things
With beauty but no soul, no life, no bloom
Of warm and breathing loveliness; the gloom
Of death was over them ; emotion's springs
Were still, and to my sad imaginings
They seemed like relics in an ancient tomb.

A woman came, and gently touched the lyre
With sympathetic tenderness, and lo—
Transfiguration breathed around, and then
The dust of death glowed with celestial fire
To life and soul and loveliness : and so
The ministrel Love transfigures earth and men.

WHENCE AND WHITHER?

I.

LIFE is a wave that comes from the unknown
Vast ocean of eternal power and thought
That, with the elements of earth inwrought,
Rolls proudly onward in the little zone
Of time and sense, with mind and feeling sown
Upon its breast, and, in its swelling, brought
To an intensity of power that ought
To fix them on an everlasting throne.

And then—the wave majestically breaks,
But stirs the shingles scattered on the shore
Of Time ; with feebler force it breaks again,
Then rolls with all the hopes and powers it bore
Back to the vast immeasurable main.

II.

When billows break and boom upon the shore,
They disappear in clouds of misty spray
That whiten all the rocks—then fade away.
A moment longer—and the answering roar
Of echoes, wakened on the ocean floor,
Has ceased, and then the wave has had its day
Of life and beauty; but with no delay,
In other forms, its force lives evermore.

So when a wave of human life and thought,
That rolls to earth from the eternal main,
Breaks on the shore, and, breaking, disappears :
The spirit that engendered it, and wrought
Such wonders with its elements, again
Takes form and lives eternal in the spheres.

THE END.

PRINTED BY WILLIAM CLOWES AND SONS, LIMITED,
LONDON AND BECCLES.